THE FLYING DUTCHMAN

Retold by Catherine Storr
Illustrated by Andrew Brown

Raintree Childrens Books
Milwaukee • Toronto • Melbourne • London
Belitha Press Limited • London

Note: The story and illustrations have been based on original historical sources. The most famous version of the story is found in *Der Fliegende Holländer,* an opera by Richard Wagner first performed in 1843.

ED

Art Director: Treld Bicknell

First published in the United States of America 1985
by Raintree Publishers Inc.
330 East Kilbourn Avenue, Milwaukee, Wisconsin 53202
in association with Belitha Press Ltd, London.

Conceived, designed and produced by Belitha Press Ltd,
2 Beresford Terrace, London N5 2DH

Library of Congress Cataloging in Publication Data

Storr, Catherine.
The flying Dutchman.

Summary: Retells the legend of the Dutch sea captain destined to sail forever over the seven seas unless he finds the love of a faithful girl.
[1. Folklore—Netherlands] I. Title.
PZ8.1.S882Fl 1985 398.2'2'09492 85-16711
ISBN 0-8172-2501-3 (lib. bdg.)
ISBN 0-8172-2509-9 (softcover)

Cover printed in the United States; body printed in Great Britain.
Bound in the United States of America.

1 2 3 4 5 6 7 8 9 89 88 87 86 85

Sailors bring back strange tales from the sea. They tell of huge sea serpents and of whirlpools, of jagged rocks and flying fish, of spouting whales and mermaids. One of the strangest tales is the tale of the ghost ship which has been sailing over the world's oceans for hundreds and hundreds of years.

Once there was a girl called Senta who lived on a rocky coast near the sea. The men in her family had always been sailors, so Senta heard all the stories about the wonders and terrors of the sea. But she had never been told the story of the ghost ship.

One day she heard two sailors talking. "Have you ever seen the ghost ship?"

"No, I haven't. But my grandfather's great-grandfather, he saw it sailing past the lighthouse there and trying to get into the harbor. When it was nearly across the bar, the wind changed and blew it out to sea again."

That evening, Senta asked her grandfather, "Grandfather, what is the ghost ship?"

At first her grandfather would not tell her, but at last he said, "It is the ship of the Flying Dutchman."

Long, long ago, there was a captain of a Dutch ship who was a proud, obstinate, clever man. He knew more than anyone about winds and tides, and he boasted that there was nowhere in the seven seas that he could not reach in his ship.

One day the Dutchman wanted to sail round the Cape of Good Hope. The wind blew strongly against him. He tried again and again, but each time, the wind blew him back. At last he cried out, "If God will not send me a fair wind, I call on the Devil. Satan, send me a wind, and ask what price you will!"

The Devil heard the Dutchman's prayer and he laughed. He sent the wind the Dutchman had prayed for, and the ship rounded the Cape of Good Hope. But with the wind, the Devil also sent a curse. The Dutchman would never be able to bring his ship to land. From that day, he and his sailors must wander over the oceans of the world, never able to set foot on solid ground. They could not rest, and they could not die.

"Will the poor Dutchman have to go on sailing forever?" Senta asked.

"Only one thing can save him," her grandfather said. "And that will never happen. Once in seven years he may land on shore and stay on land for one day and night. If he could find a girl to love him in that short time, he would be saved. But he has never found such a girl and never will."

"I would! I would love him!" Senta said.

"Nonsense! You are a child. You should pray that you may never see the ghost ship and her terrible captain."

Senta thought, "I am not like other girls. I would love the Flying Dutchman. I would rescue him from the Devil's curse." She had always loved looking at the sea. She loved seeing the great ships sailing into the harbor.

She loved sitting on the high cliffs and seeing the waves break on the rocks below. Now she liked to watch the curving rim where the sea meets the sky, as she sat waiting for the ghost ship to appear, with its old, tattered sails and its old, weary crew.

One day, as she sat on the cliff, she saw a strange ship in the distance. It was a sailing ship of an old-fashioned kind. As it drew nearer, Senta saw that the sails were in tatters and the sailors were old, old men, thin and stiff, like ghosts. The ship sailed straight toward the harbor, past the lighthouse, and over the harbor bar.

Senta ran down to the harbor and called out to the sailors there, "A strange ship is sailing in!"

The sailors looked out and saw the ship. "I've never seen her like before," said one.

"She is rigged in the fashion of three hundred years ago," said another.

The ship drew nearer. "It is the ghost ship!" someone cried. At once they all fled. The harbor was left empty. Only Senta watched the ship come to land.

She saw the old, weary sailormen tie up the ship's ropes to the quay. She saw their tired eyes, she saw their hands, worn and sore with handling the ship's ropes for hundreds of years. Then she saw the ship's captain, the Dutchman. He was tall, with a black beard and black hair. His face was pale and haunted, the face of a man who has made a pact with the Devil.

"I could love him, and save him," Senta thought. But she was still a child.

The next day, Senta went down to the harbor, but the strange ship had gone. No one would talk about it, but Senta's grandfather said, "It will be seven years before the Dutchman tries to land again. By that time, I shall be dead."

The seven years passed slowly by. Senta was no longer a child. She was a beautiful young woman. Several young men wanted to marry her, but Senta refused them all.

At last, one evening as she sat at her spinning wheel in her father's house, she heard a cry from the harbor. A strange ship was sailing in, and as it came, thunder roared, lightning split the sky, and a furious gust of wind blew the ship over the harbor bar.

Presently, Senta's father came back from the harbor. He brought with him a tall, pale man with black hair and a black beard. Senta knew at once who this man was. She left her spinning wheel and said, "Last time you were here, I was only a child!"

"Are you afraid of me?" the Dutchman asked.

I am not afraid. I have been waiting for you. If you will let me, I will love you," Senta said.

"You don't know who I am," the Dutchman said.

"Yes, I do. You are the Flying Dutchman."

"Are you not afraid of me? You know that I am cursed by the Devil?"

Senta said, "I know. But if you let me love you, you would be free from the Devil's curse."

When Senta said this the Dutchman turned toward the open door. He cried out, "Do you hear this, Satan? I have found a woman to love me. Now release me from my bargain. Set me free!"

A jagged flash of lightning pierced the dark sky. The sea below the cliffs boiled and heaved. Thunder rumbled; the houses in the little port trembled and shook.

Some people say that Senta's love saved the Dutchman. Others say that the Devil would not give up his prey. There are some old sailors who insist that the ghost ship can still be seen, sailing with ragged sails and a crew of the dead, over the seven seas, forever and ever, from now until eternity.